A FIREFLY BOOK

Published by Firefly Books Ltd. 2017

First printing

Publisher Cataloging-in-Publication Data (U.S.)

Library of Congress Cataloging-in-Publication Data is available

Library and Archives Canada Cataloguing in Publication

Solotareff, Grégoire
[Dictionnaire des sorcières. English]
        Dictionary of witches / Grégoire Solotareff.
Translation of: Dictionnaire des sorcières.
ISBN 978-1-77085-995-1 (softcover)
        1. Witches--Dictionaries, Juvenile. 2. Witchcraft--
Dictionaries, Juvenile. I. Title. II. Title: Dictionnaire
des sorcières. English.
BF1566.S6513 2017   133.4'303   C2017-902055-2

Published in the United States by
Firefly Books (U.S.) Inc.
P.O. Box 1338, Ellicott Station
Buffalo, New York 14205

Published in Canada by
Firefly Books Ltd.
50 Staples Avenue, Unit 1
Richmond Hill, Ontario L4B 0A7

Translator: Claudine Mersereau
Editor: Michael Worek

Printed in China

To all the witches, you know who you are.

Thank you to Margaux Duroux and Louise Colomb for their precious help.

We acknowledge the financial support of the Government of Canada.

Grégoire Solotareff

DICTIONARY OF
WITCHES

FIREFLY BOOKS

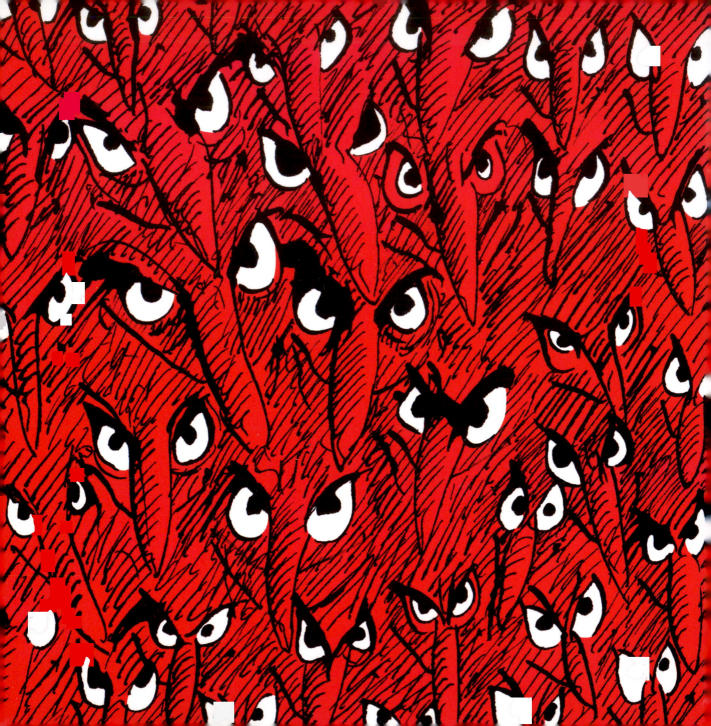

CONTENTS

ABRACADABRA

To calm down difficult children,
witches say a secret
and magical word: "Abracadabra!"
It comes from an expression in the witches' language,
"Embrace a cadaver," which means
"to hold up a dead body in your arms."
In other words, consider what to do next.

AIR SICKNESS

In winter, gale force winds make witches, who are already prone to air sickness despite the powers of their brooms, look even less well.

AMULETS

Witches always keep at least one or two boxes
of amulets with them, just in case.

AN INTERESTING IDEA

If you're not sure what to give a friend for Christmas,
here is an interesting idea, also called "The Witch's Test":
Catch a nice, fat rat, put it into a shoe box
and then give it to your friend.
If your friend is delighted when she opens her gift,
you know what your friend is.

APPETIZER

In the witches' language, chicks, bunny rabbits and chickadees are called "appetizers," and older witches sometimes call them "nibbles."

BABIES

Bats are mice that sometime fly
and from which witches have taken
the fur to glue onto the heads of babies
who were born bald.
(See "Hair.")

BIG

When a witch cackles,
big is her mouth and
dark are her thoughts.

BIG MEANIE

We often call someone a "witch" when,
in fact, the person is simply a big meanie.
Here is the difference:
There will never be a "Dictionary of Big Meanies."

BITE

Witches grow up in the hollow trunks of old trees,
in the dirt and dampness.
Their first toys are bugs and worms.
Thanks to the pointy teeth they have from birth,
they can also bite them for fun or even eat them.

BOO!

When it's windy, you can really see the difference
between a fairy and a witch:
Under her coat covered in precious jewels,
a fairy's dress or slip is always
clean and colorful, while those of a witch —
oh my!

CABBAGE, PEBBLE, OWL, KNEE, FLEA

These are five words that witches use all the time
because they often have fleas, always have knees,
sometimes owl eyes and pebble teeth,
and they often eat cabbage
(that's why they fart a lot).

CHICKEN

Many witches dream of opening a restaurant.
But it would be best if they put chicken in their
sandwiches instead of what they usually use.

CHRISTMAS DINNER

Christmas dinner for eight witches:
Take a medium-sized knot of snakes
(they are easy to catch).
Stuff the snakes with six crushed toads
(the snakes might put up a bit of a fuss).
Heat the oven to 400°F.
Bake for one hour while plugging your nose.
Let cool slightly
(remembering to keep your nose plugged).

COLOR

Witches do not consider black a color,
which is false,
but witches aren't artists,
so it is best that they keep quiet on the subject.

CONSCIENTIOUSLY

In a forest, you must always build your cabin conscientiously. For example, don't let the branches extend past your general structure, since a neighboring witch will always check that it's well built.

CONTRARY

Contrary to witches who only sometimes have some,
old men always have nose hair.
(Look closely!)

DANG!

When a young witch stumbles
in her too-big shoes,
she doesn't say "dang!",
but another terrible word that has
erased itself from this book by magic.

DEVIL'S FOOD

There is no reason to call a cake "witch's foot"
since no one would buy it,
even if it was delicious.

DIFFICULT

The witches' favorite number is four
because there are four seasons,
four elements, four compass points
and four eternal truths,
but mostly because
it's the gymnastics move they like best
because it's the most difficult.

DINNER

Witches own only one book,
their book of spells,
which can seem amusing
but is actually hard to read and very boring.

This is why...
1. witches never read their book;
2. witches are very ignorant;
3. it's best not to invite a witch to dinner,
   since she would have nothing to talk about.

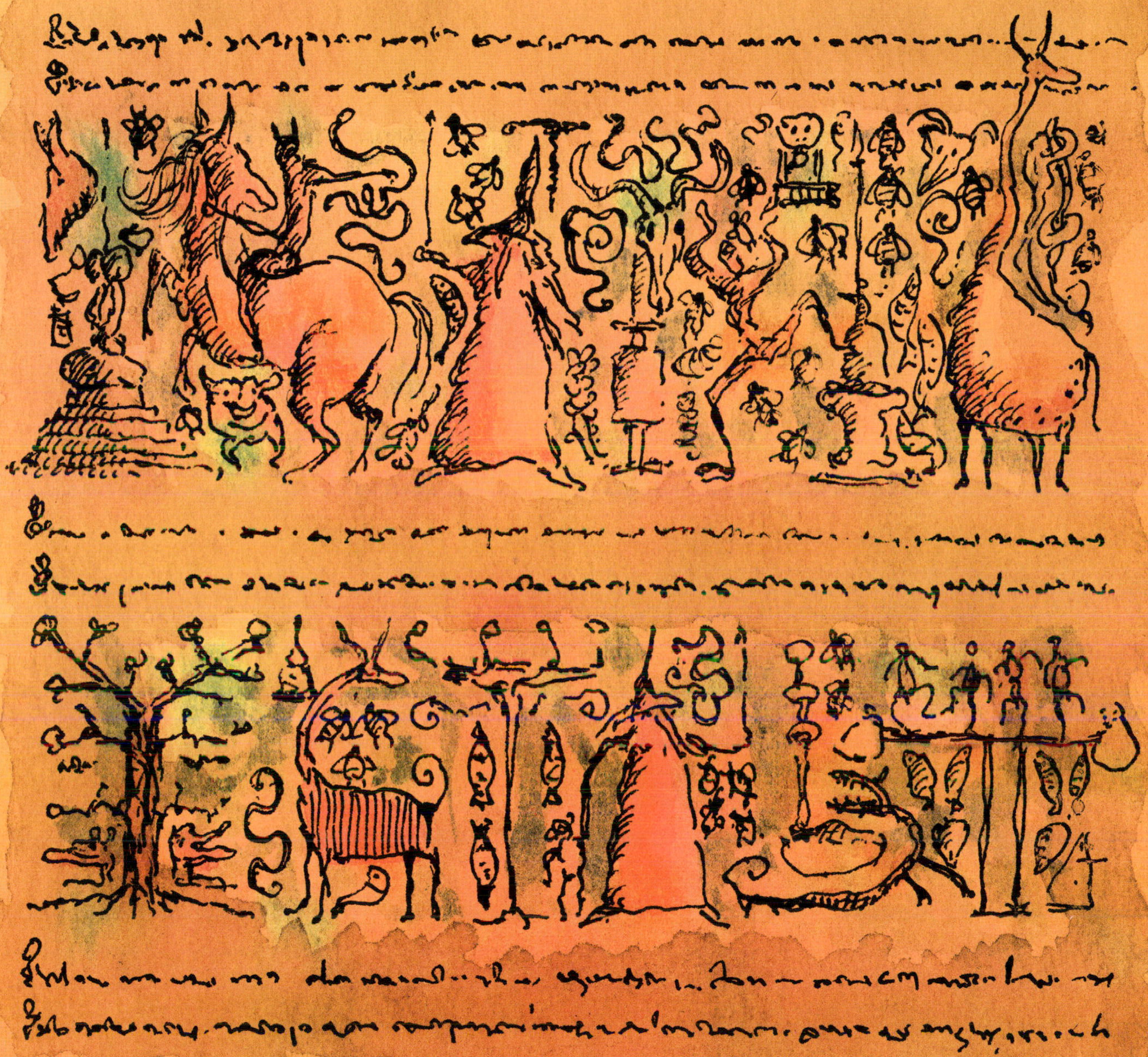

DISGUSTING

Even though the ice cream flavors
witches like best are the most disgusting,
they take great pleasure in licking them
since witches are also disgusting.

DROPPINGS

Witches sometimes invite their friends over for tea.

On these occasions, they serve them cakes

made of bird droppings,

which aren't very appetizing and,

moreover, are not very good.

They do this as a test of friendship.

EARTHWORMS

A pretty easy snack recipe for witches:
Take an earthworm,
put it in a pot of earth,
add to it a cup of snail slime
(you'll need a little patience for this part),
sprinkle well with sugar.
Eat.

EVERYDAY

Well made and usually in a pretty color,
a witch's everyday shoes
are nothing more
than ordinary pumps.

EVERYWHERE

On roofs in all the cities of the world,
there are the tracks of witches,
more or less fresh and more or less visible,
because witches are all over and everywhere.

EVIL EYE

There is a big difference between
the evil eye and an evil look.
The evil eye (in other words, a lot of trouble)
is a ridiculous belief and doesn't exist,
while an evil look, or "witchy face," is quite common.
(You just have to take the subway
 in rush hour to realize this.)

EYES

In a witch's stew,
there are always beautiful circles of grease
that float on the surface and look like their eyes.

FACE

Talk about ghosts with a witch,
and you'll see the face she makes!

FEW

All that is required is a few hairs on her chin
and there is (almost) nothing to distinguish
a witch from a wizard.

FIGHTING

The big bad wolf is a witch's main rival:

He scares children and never makes them laugh.

This is why witches and the big bad wolf often fight.

GIFTED

Witches are gifted at many things,
but not at making flower bouquets.
But then, who would they give the flowers to?

GO FIGURE!

For witches, night is day,
but day can't be made into night.

GOOSE POOP

The colors that witches like in particular are:
sooty, brown, slate, copper, cauldron, rust, ruddy,
maw red, blood red, violet-ish, yellowish,
olive-ish, bluish, earthy, pallid, livid, gloomy,
pigeon throat, crimson, dead leaf, ochre, flea,
and goose poop.

GUESSING GAME NO. 1

If you see two witches from behind,
how do you know that it's not a witch and a wizard?
Answer: You turn the page.

GUESSING GAME NO. 2

If, once you've turned the page, you see two witches head on, how can you be sure it's not actually a couple of wizards?
Answer: There is no way of knowing (and it's not very important).

HAIR

Some owls are trained by witches to bring them mice,
whose fur they shave off their heads
(thus turning them into bald bats).
Then, with the help of their super-sticky saliva,
they stick the fur on babies
who have too little hair at birth.

HAIRDO

Contrary to what you might think, witches
do style their hair, but they style it "like a witch,"
meaning not with a brush but with a broom
(for chimneys, for example), which gives their hair
its trademark color and can also give the impression
that they do not style their hair at all.

HAPPILY

Witches don't have babies.
Happily!

HAZEL

The eyes of witches are often hazel,
in other words, not brown, not blue, not green.
And when we talk of witches having hazel eyes,
you understand the meaning of "witch hazel."

HEEL

Mayflies are poor little innocent flies that witches
like to cruelly crush under their heel
even though they don't sting!

HOOT

Girls sometimes say that being a witch must be "a hoot."
Curious expression, since owls which hoot,
don't like witches at all.
They scare away the children that the owls do like.

IMAGINING

They try to make us think that witches, kings,
presidents and cabinet ministers
never go to the bathroom.
That's not true.
Seeing them there isn't funny,
but imagining them there is.

KIND

It is very easy to know if someone is,
deep down inside, nice.
You just need to look into their eyes.
You're usually right.

KQDWXGJDFTN-PMTRVSKLGQTFPZ

Certain witches can be bewitched —
and therefore neutralized — by more powerful witches
(luckily, otherwise we'd be invaded!)
with the help of magical spells such as
"kqdwxgjdftnpmtrvsklgptfpz!"

LAUGHING

Why do old rabbits love witches?
Because witches make them laugh
when they try to catch them.

LAVENDER

On Sunday, witches like to dress in lavender
because they find that this color goes particularly well
with their complexion when they're well rested.

LIKE

Witches don't like anyone,
not even rats,
even though they are very likeable animals,
once you get to know them.

LOVE

A potion is a kind of juice prepared with love
and used by witches for different purposes:
cooking, magic, wickedness
or all three at the same time.

MAGICAL

We use the word "magical"
to describe landscapes with fog, snow or sunsets,
because it is witches who are responsible for them,
and if witches didn't exist,
these landscapes would be of no interest.

MAGICIAN

Is Santa Claus a kind of magician,
or are magicians a kind of Santa Claus?

MARRY

Sorcerers, when asked certain indiscreet questions,
will defend themselves by saying that
"it's better not to marry anyone than to marry a witch,"
but we know that witches never marry.
And we know why.

MISTAKE

When you see someone's face
with a nose that's a bit too long
and with things moving beneath —
make no mistake —
That's a witch.

MISTER WITCH

There are male witches,
just like there are male frogs or female mayors.
They are referred to as Mister Witch,
just as we say Mister Frog
or Madam Mayor.

MUSLIN

The fabric from which witches' hats are sewn
is called muslin. It is usually purple.
(It's also the name of a very nice
dragon-tailed fairy that is,
unfortunately, extinct.)

NASTY

Certain cats sometimes accompany witches
on their evening strolls
in order to learn how to transform
nasty people into mice or rats.

NEVER

Witches' hands have a particular feature:
When you shake their hand, you stay stuck.
This is why you never, ever read a story about
someone shaking hands with a witch.

NONSENSE

As the witches' nocturnal confidants,
lizards often like to settle themselves
comfortably in the sun to rest in the morning,
since they've had enough,
having heard nonsense all night long.

NORMAL

There's nothing special about witches' brooms;
everybody's familiar with them.
They are made of wood and straw
and sweep completely normally.

NOTHING

When you encounter a witch in the dark,
you see practically nothing.

OBSERVE

When a rabbit looks at you in a slightly weird way,
take advantage of the situation to observe it
and take note of any small details that
could help you figure out if it's actually
a witch disguised as a rabbit.
Beware!

PEANUTS

The slugs, even the very big ones,
that witches eat (usually raw)
are like peanuts for them.
But usually neither peanuts
nor slugs are eaten raw!

POOR

If you think "Oh! That poor cat!"
when seeing a cat, you should ask
yourselves if it's a witch's cat, because
they only act unhappy so that they will be well fed
and be able to do as they please.

PRETTY

A witch could be pretty.
Beautiful, even.
She can wear a pretty dress and a pretty hat,
which is disturbing because
we might not see that she's a witch.
But this is rare.

REAL

It is said that witches always have black cats,
but this isn't true.
It's actually the black cats that always have witches,
whom they visit from time to time.

ROCKET SCIENCE

Drawing a witch isn't rocket science!
(Timed drawing, finished in seventeen seconds,
twenty-eight one hundredths.)

SALIVA

Witches have sticky green saliva which gives them:
1. bad breath,
2. a bad temper,
3. an unfriendly side (especially when they drool) and
4. a pretty tongue.

SCOWL

Elephants never scowl.
Except when they see witches
flying a bit too low.

SECOND HOME

Some caves are used by witches as second homes.
That's why we also call them "second homes for witches."
At the entrance to these caves,
even the plants are awful.
The soil can also be ugly.
Sometimes even the sky is just unbelievable!

SHADOW

Witches have a shadow, like everyone else,
since there isn't a shadow of a doubt that they exist.
Otherwise, we would never speak of them
and even less about their shadows.

SHOES

Dirty, pointy, thorny, too big and often worn out,
a witch's evening shoes are made in hell.

SIDEKICKS

Is it really surprising that crows, like owls, are witches' sidekicks?

SPECIAL

A witch's house isn't particularly special,
other than the fact that you wouldn't live in it
for all the money in the world.

SPELL

Anyone can cast a spell on a witch.
All you need to do is eat a live toad
right before meeting a witch.

STILL

We say that a witch is still young
when she positions herself on her broom
so she can fly as quickly as possible.
Older witches don't care,
and they position themselves more comfortably.

STUPID

If someone steals your vacuum one day,
especially if they steal it from the closet,
you can be sure that a stupid witch did it because
they think that vacuums have now replaced brooms.
But this appliance has no chance of flying.

TALISMAN

A talisman is an object that apparently
has the power to bring happiness.
However, witches' talismans are often disgusting
objects with feathers glued onto dried fish guts,
a bit like their amulets.
(See "Amulets.")

TEETH

If you want to have teeth and breath
like a witch, there is only one way to do it:
don't brush your teeth before going to bed.
It works!

TICKLES

Being tickled by a witch isn't much fun
and doesn't really tickle, since their long
and sometimes forked fingernails scratch you,
which is a bit unpleasant and is nothing like
being tickled by your parents,
which mostly makes you laugh.

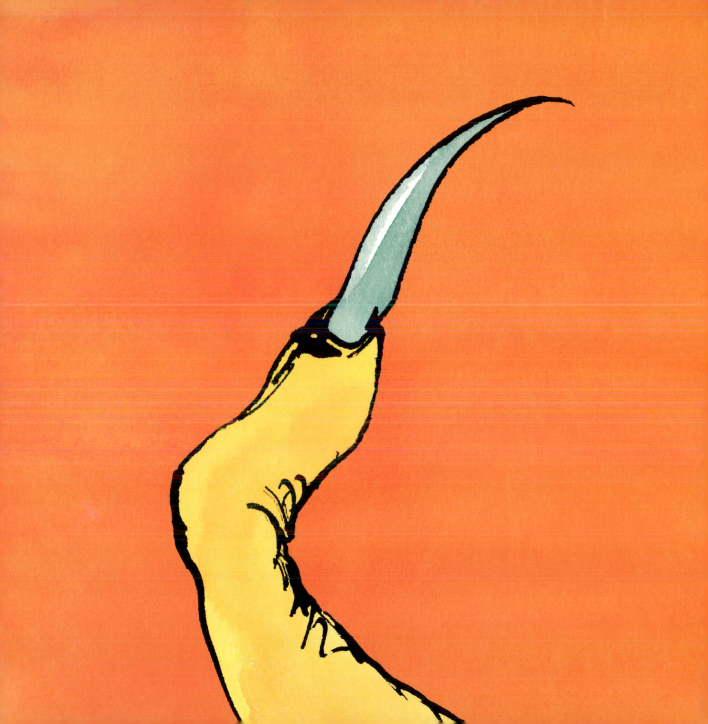

TRAIN

When you see a train all lit up and, seemingly
without an engine, go by in the night,
it is either an RET (Regional ExpressTrain)
or an SMT (Secret Magic Train)
filled with witches heading to a convention.
(The SMT is, in fact, no longer a secret
at all since we saw it.)

TRANSFORM

A bad thought directed at a person
or even a nice animal is called a "spell."
It can go as far as completely
transforming that person.

UNCLEAR

Witches are neither blonde nor brunette
nor redheaded nor auburn.
Their hair is a rather unclear color that,
curiously, adds to their charm.

UNCERTAIN

The power of a witch is uncertain.
For example, if you ask her to turn you into a prince,
you have a better chance of becoming a toad.
That's the reason why there are a lot more toads
than there are princes.

UNHAPPY

Witches' dogs are always nice and never bite
since witches don't forbid them from doing anything.
Curiously enough, fairies' dogs are
very polite but quite unhappy.
Because they are brought up so strictly,
they are usually mean.

WHITE

There are witches
who are rather young and rather slim
and like to put a white sheet over their heads
and fly around without their brooms.
They call themselves "ghosts."

WHY

Why do children
like witches even though witches
1. are not very nice and
2. want to kidnap and
3. eat them?
There isn't, to this day,
an answer to this question.

WICKED

The trolls who help witches
— who resemble witches, as do certain cats
and even certain people —
are more foolish than wicked.
Though the witches don't treat them very nicely,
they stay under the witches' control
even though they could run away.

XANTHIA

Witches' best friends are called xanthia.
You've often seen them without knowing
what they were called or where they were going
(a bit like people passing you in the street).
They are little light brown moths
that are very nice and very friendly.

YOUNG

Like anyone else,
a witch can look ridiculous
if she wears dresses that are too short
when she is no longer very young.